GLOW-IN-THE-DARK WINGS!

MEGABATICORE
CHIROPTERA LUMINOSA GIGANTEOMONSTRUM

- FLIGHT SPEED UP TO 35 MILES PER HOUR
- EATS 4 POUNDS OF INSECTS A DAY
- DOUBLES AS A NIGHTLIGHT!

MIMETIC SKIN

CYCLOPTUPUS
OCTOPODA CYCLOCEPHALOMONSTRUM

- SQUIRTS UP TO 2 GALLONS OF INK
- FITS IN SMALL SPACES
- EXPERT AT HIDE-AND-SEEK!

*DESIGNER MONSTERS & CO. NOT RESPONSIBLE FOR MONSTERS OR THEIR MESSES AFTER PURCHASE.

To Mom, for always putting up with my monkey business. —S. F.

To my mom and my brothers, with all my love. —C. R.

STERLING CHILDREN'S BOOKS
New York

An Imprint of Sterling Publishing Co., Inc.
1166 Avenue of the Americas
New York, NY 10036

STERLING CHILDREN'S BOOKS and the distinctive Sterling Children's Books logo
are trademarks of Sterling Publishing Co., Inc.

Text © 2017 Sue Fliess

Illustrations © 2017 Claudia Ranucci

ISBN 978-1-4549-1894-3

Distributed in Canada by Sterling Publishing
c/o Canadian Manda Group, 664 Annette Street
Toronto, Ontario, Canada M6S 2C8
Distributed in the United Kingdom by GMC Distribution Services
Castle Place, 166 High Street, Lewes, East Sussex, England BN7 1XU
Distributed in Australia by NewSouth Books, 45 Beach Street, Coogee, NSW 2034, Australia

For information about custom editions, special sales, and premium and corporate purchases,
please contact Sterling Special Sales at 800-805-5489 or specialsales@sterlingpublishing.com.

Manufactured in China

Lot #:
2 4 6 8 10 9 7 5 3 1
07/17

sterlingpublishing.com

Design by Heather Kelly

The artwork for this book was created digitally.

We Wish for a
MONSTER
CHRISTMAS

by **Sue Fliess**
illustrated by **Claudia Ranucci**

STERLING CHILDREN'S BOOKS
New York

We wish for a furry monster,

a big, hairy, scary monster,

our own stomping, chomping monster, for Christmas this year.

Our friends all will get to know him,

and over the snow we'll tow him,

we'll take him to school and show him
there's nothing to fear.

He'll eat all our peas.

We'll check him for fleas.

He'll hang by his knees from
the brass chandelier.

Our dad says we cannot buy one,
or rent one, or even try one.

But WE know a guy who'll fly one
of those monsters right here.

We asked Santa Claus
to help with our cause.

MEET SANTA!

"Okay, you may have one—
you've been good all year!"

Our mom took up meditation.
Our dad hollered in frustration.

But we had a celebration with monsterly cheer!

Our monster is causing trouble.
Request backup on the double!
The playroom has turned to rubble,
which we have to clear.

He's making a mess
and causing us stress.
He's using Mom's dress as a tissue . . . oh, dear!

He ate every chair and table.

He chewed through the TV cable.

So Dad says we won't be able
to keep him in here.

We brainstormed all day
and found a great way
for our monster to stay
without being too near.

He now lives out in the backyard
and makes a terrific night guard.

See, owning a monster's not hard
when you've got the gear!

We sure love our furry monster,

our big, hairy, scary monster,

our own stomping, chomping monster.

But here's an idea . . .

We'll wish for a bunch of monkeys,
our own silly, screeching monkeys,
just five hundred swinging monkeys . . .

... for Christmas next year!

CHANGES COLOR IN SUNLIGHT!

HOWLING SPIDER MONKEY
ATELES FUSCICEPS HOWLUS

- HOWLS EARLY IN THE MORNING—YOU WON'T NEED AN ALARM CLOCK!
- EATS LEAVES AND INSECTS FROM YOUR GARDEN
- PREHENSILE TAIL TO HELP CARRY GROCERIES!

EXTRA LONG TAIL!

DESIGNER MONKEYS!*

HURRY, WHILE SUPPLIES LAST! ORDER NOW FOR DISCOUNTS ON YOUR NEXT ORDER!

RAINBOW LION TAMARIN
LEONTOPITHECUS RAINBOWLIA

- ROARS LIKE A LION
- GREAT CLIMBER
- CAN PICK YOUR OUT-OF-REACH PERSIMMONS!